In loving memory of Betty O'Rourke
J.W.

For Agata and Magda
S.F-D.

First published 2011 by Walker Books Ltd
87 Vauxhall Walk, London SE11 5HJ

2 4 6 8 10 9 7 5 3 1

Text © 2011 Jeanne Willis
Illustrations © 2011 Sarah Fox-Davies
The right of Jeanne Willis and Sarah Fox-Davies to be identified
as author and illustrator respectively of this work has been asserted by them
in accordance with the Copyright, Designs and Patents Act 1988

This book has been typeset in Quercus

Printed in China

British Library Cataloguing in Publication Data:
a catalogue record for this book is available from the British Library

ISBN 978-1-4063-0474-9

www.walker.co.uk

Mole's
Sunrise

Jeanne Willis　　Sarah Fox-Davies

WALKER BOOKS
AND SUBSIDIARIES

LONDON · BOSTON · SYDNEY · AUCKLAND

Vole got up just before dawn.
Mole was eating breakfast
but Vole didn't have time.
"Where are you off to in such a hurry?"
asked Mole.
"I want to see the sunrise," said Vole.

Mole had never seen the sunrise.

"It's beautiful," said Vole.

"I'd love to see it," said Mole.

"Come with me," said Vole.

Off they went, hand in hand.

"Are we going very far?" asked Mole.

"Only down to the lake," said Vole.

"It's the best place. Mind that tree root, Mole."

Mole felt the damp mist in his fur.

He heard the crackle of leaves under his feet.

Mole sniffed the air. He could smell the lake.

"We're here," he said.

"Let's sit on the log with the others," said Vole.

"What others?" asked Mole.

There was Rabbit, Squirrel and Sparrow.

Mole and Vole sat with them.

"We've come to see the sunrise," said Vole.

"So have we," said Rabbit.

"I hear it's very beautiful," said Mole.

"I should say so," said Squirrel.

"Here comes the sun!" said Vole.
"I can just see the top of its head.
It's like the soft yolk of a fried egg."
Like the one I eat for breakfast,
thought Mole.

"It's rising higher," said Rabbit.
"It's up to its middle.
It's sizzling in the lake like an egg
in a pan of butter. Now it's burst!
It's dripping hot, runny sunny stuff everywhere."
"That's what happened to my egg!" said Mole.
He wiped the yolk off his waistcoat.

The sun rose right out of the lake.
"Now the clouds are like scoops
of raspberry ice cream," said Rabbit.
"And blueberry!" added Vole,
"swirled with steaming custard."
"Delicious!" said Mole, who always
swirled custard on his ice cream.

The sun rose higher and higher.
"Now it reminds me of a shiny gold
button," said Squirrel.
Mole felt the shiny gold button
on his waistcoat.
The sun was like that,
only a zillion times bigger.
Or so everybody said.
"It only looks as small as a button
because it's so far away," said Vole.

Sparrow said the sun was hotter
than the hottest fire.
"It's so hot, it's melting
the moody clouds," he said. "It's made
them as light and fluffy
as feather down."
Mole felt Sparrow's soft feathers.
"I get the picture," he said.

The sun had risen.

"So that's what the sunrise looks like,"
said Mole. "Thank you for showing it to me.
I never knew it was so beautiful."

Mole was blind but at last he'd seen the sunrise.

He didn't see it with his eyes; he saw it in his mind.

And it was even more beautiful

than anyone could imagine.